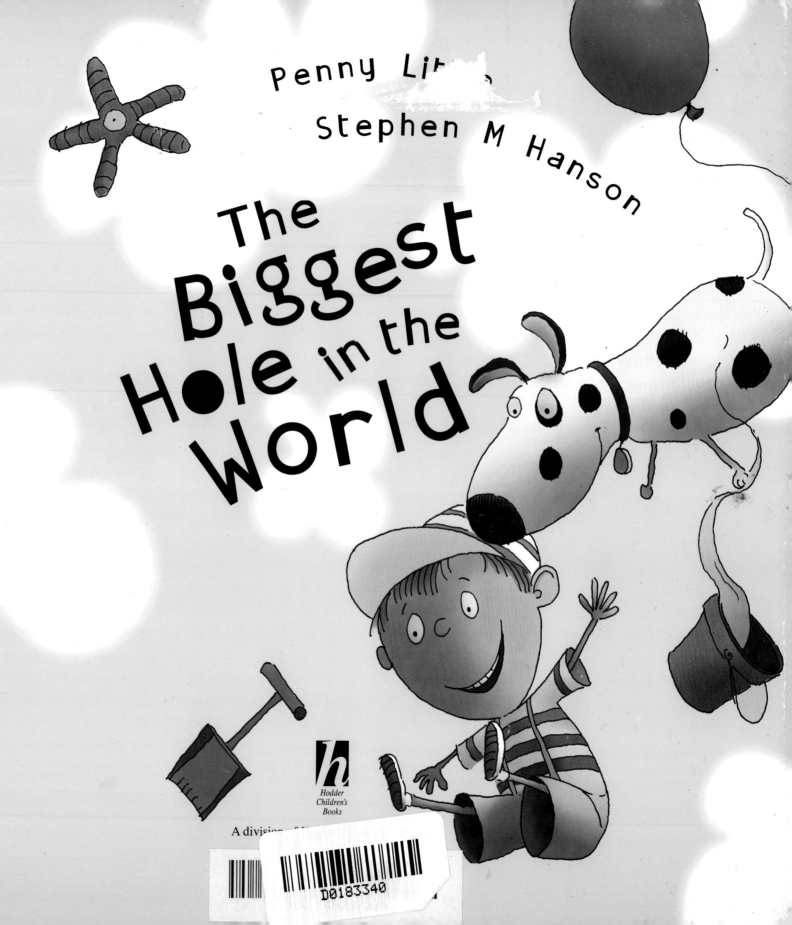

Penny Li...

Stephen M Hanson

The Biggest Hole in the World

Hodder
Children's
Books

A division of...

D0183340

Charlie and his dad had packed a picnic with crisps and cakes. On the way to the seaside with Doggo they sang songs in the car and Dad told nail-biting stories of wicked pirates and scary sea monsters. When they got there, Charlie started to dig.

It was hard work;

dig, dig, dig.